IBTIHAJ MUHAMMAD

OLYMPIC FENCER

KATIE LAJINESS

Big Buddy Books
An Imprint of Abdo Publishing
abdopublishing.com

BIG BUDDY OLYMPIC BIOGRAPHIES

abdopublishing.com

Published by Abdo Publishing, a division of ABDO, PO Box 398166, Minneapolis, Minnesota 55439.

Big Buddy Books™ is a trademark and logo of Abdo Publishing.

Printed in the United States of America, North Mankato, Minnesota.
102016
012017

THIS BOOK CONTAINS RECYCLED MATERIALS

Cover Photo: ASSOCIATED PRESS
Interior Photos: Alireza Teimoury/Alamy Stock Photo (p. 9); ASSOCIATED PRESS (pp. 11, 19, 21, 23, 25, 31); © Bruce Cotler/Globe Photos/ZUMA Wire/Alamy Live News (p. 5); D Dipasupil/Contributor/ Getty Images (p. 27); epa european pressphoto agency b.v./Alamy Stock Photo (p. 29); © IStockphoto.com (p. 15); ITAR-TASS Photo Agency/Alamy Stock Photo (p. 17); REUTERS/Alamy Stock Photo (p. 13); Xinhua/Alamy Stock Photo (p. 23).

Coordinating Series Editor: Tamara L. Britton
Graphic Design: Jenny Christensen

Publisher's Cataloging-in-Publication Data

Names: Lajiness, Katie, author.
Title: Ibtihaj Muhammad / by Katie Lajiness.
Description: Minneapolis, MN : Abdo Publishing, 2017. | Series: Big buddy Olympic biographies | Includes bibliographical references and index.
Identifiers: LCCN 2016953149 | ISBN 9781680785548 (lib. bdg.) | ISBN 9781680785821 (ebook)
Subjects: LCSH: Muhammad, Ibtihaj, 1985- --Juvenile literature. | Fencing--United States--Biography--Juvenile literature. | Women Olympic athletes--United States--Biography--Juvenile literature. | Olympic Games (31st : 2016 : Rio de Janeiro, Brazil)
Classification: DDC 796.86/092 [B]--dc23
LC record available at http://lccn.loc.gov/2016953149

CONTENTS

ROLE MODEL

Ibtihaj Muhammad (IHB-tee-hahj moh-HA-muhd) is a famous fencer. Fencing is a sport in which two players fight with **swords**.

Ibtihaj is a role model for young women. She is a **Muslim** sportswoman. So, Ibtihaj balances her love of sports with her religion.

SNAPSHOT

NAME:
Ibtihaj Muhammad

BIRTHDAY:
December 4, 1985

BIRTHPLACE:
Maplewood, New Jersey

TURNED PROFESSIONAL:
2007

OLYMPIC MEDALS WON:
1 bronze

CHAMPIONSHIPS:
Senior World Team Championships and World Cup

FAMILY TIES

Ibtihaj Muhammad was born in Maplewood, New Jersey, on December 4, 1985. Her parents are Eugene and Denise Muhammad. Ibtihaj has four **siblings**.

Religion is important to her family. Like many **Muslims**, she prays five times per day. And, she doesn't eat from sunrise to sunset during a holiday called Ramadan.

DID YOU KNOW?

Ibtihaj is a Muslim name that means *joy*. Her friends call her Ibti.

WHERE IN THE WORLD?

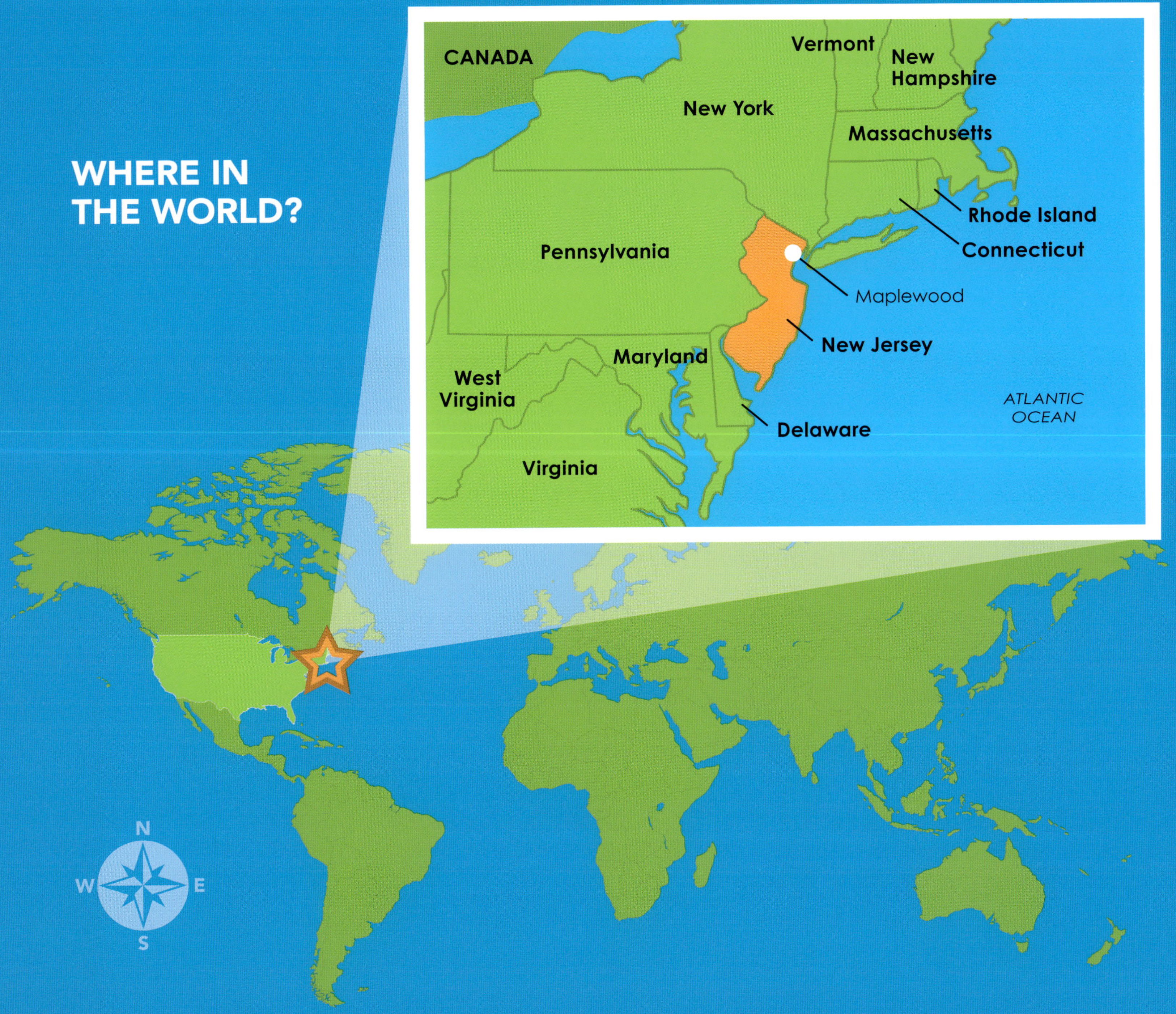

EARLY YEARS

As a **Muslim**, Ibtihaj covers her head, arms, and legs. Sadly when she was young, kids teased her for wearing a **hijab**. And, Ibtihaj's clothes made her stand out while playing volleyball, softball, and tennis.

One day, Ibtihaj and her mother saw a local fencing team practice. Fencing fit their family's values because the players were fully covered.

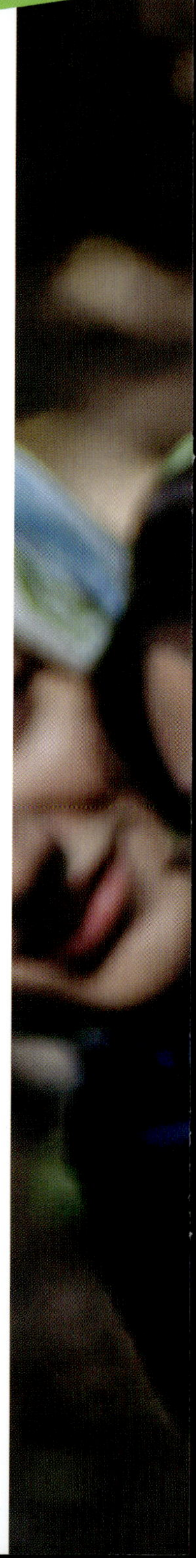

Millions of Muslim women and girls around the world cover their hair. Many wear hijabs that are bright colors to match their clothes.

STARTING OUT

When she was 13, Ibtihaj joined her first fencing team. She soon grew to love the sport.

First, Ibtihaj used a **sword** called an épée (EH-pay). As her skills improved, she began using a saber. The saber is the fastest sword for fencing.

Fencers wear a face mask to protect themselves during a match. Swords have a guard to protect one hand.

In high school, Ibtihaj joined the Peter Westbrook **Foundation**. There, she practiced her fencing skills with new **coaches**.

Ibtihaj was the captain of her high school fencing team for two years. She led the team to two state **championships**. Ibtihaj hoped fencing was a way to earn a college **scholarship**.

Students of the Peter Westbrook Foundation practice in New York City, New York.

A BIG DREAM

Ibtihaj's dream came true! She received a **scholarship** to attend Duke University in Durham, North Carolina.

Throughout college, Ibtihaj continued to train hard. In 2005, she became a Junior Olympic **champion**. Two years later, she graduated from Duke.

DID YOU KNOW?

Duke's fencing program has had two national champions and 21 All-Americans.

At Duke University, Ibtihaj was a three-time All-American.

In 2010, Ibtihaj joined the US fencing team. Sadly, a hand injury kept her from the 2012 Olympics in London, England.

But, Ibtihaj did not give up. In 2014, she became the Senior World Team **champion**. And, she won five Senior World Team **medals**.

DID YOU KNOW?

In 2012, the Muslim Women's Sport Foundation named Ibtihaj the Muslim Sportswoman of the Year.

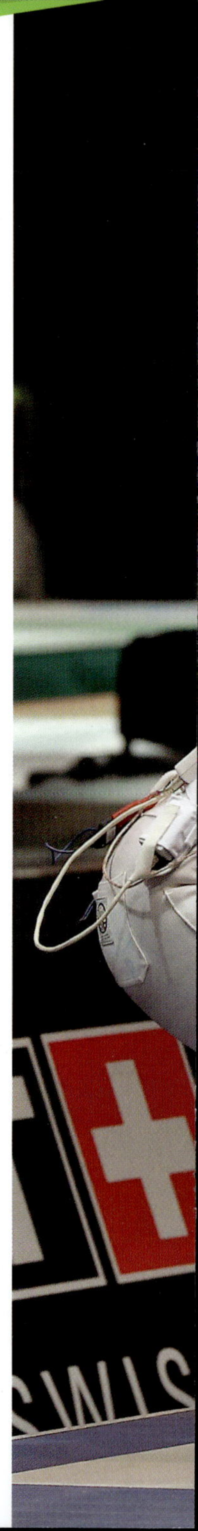

In 2014, Ibtihaj (*second from right*) and the US Women's Fencing Team went to the World Fencing Championships. They won the team saber event.

ROAD TO THE OLYMPICS

DID YOU KNOW?

Ibtihaj continues to fence during Ramadan. She trains seven hours a day without food or water.

Ibtihaj enjoyed much success by 2016. She earned bronze **medals** at the World Cup. That year, Ibtihaj was the number-two female player in the United States. At one point, she was the seventh-best female player in the world. Her success made her a good fit for the Olympic team.

In 2015, Ibtihaj and her teammates went to the Pan Am Games in Toronto, Ontario. They won gold in the team saber event.

OLYMPIC CHAMPION

Ibtihaj made history at the 2016 Olympics! She was the first American woman to wear a **hijab** in the Olympics.

In Rio de Janeiro, Brazil, Ibtihaj won the first round in the individual saber event. But, she lost the second round. Ibtihaj did not lose hope. She still had a chance to win a **medal** in the team event.

Ibtihaj was honored to greet her fans at the Olympics. They cheered on team USA during the women's team saber event.

Ibtihaj and her teammates beat Italy in the team saber event to win the bronze **medal**. She became the first **Muslim**-American woman to win an Olympic medal!

DID YOU KNOW?

In 2016, Ibtihaj met President Obama and First Lady Michelle Obama.

Italy's Rossella Gregorio (*left*) and Ibtihaj competed against each other at the Olympics.

Dagmara Wozniak (*left*), Ibtihaj (*second from left*), Monica Aksamit (*second from right*), and Mariel Zagunis (*right*) won a bronze medal in the women's team saber fencing competition.

OFF THE STRIP

Ibtihaj is busy. She practices every day to improve her speed, agility, and strength. She also travels around the world to give speeches about the benefits of sports. Ibtihaj wants other **Muslim** girls to love playing sports.

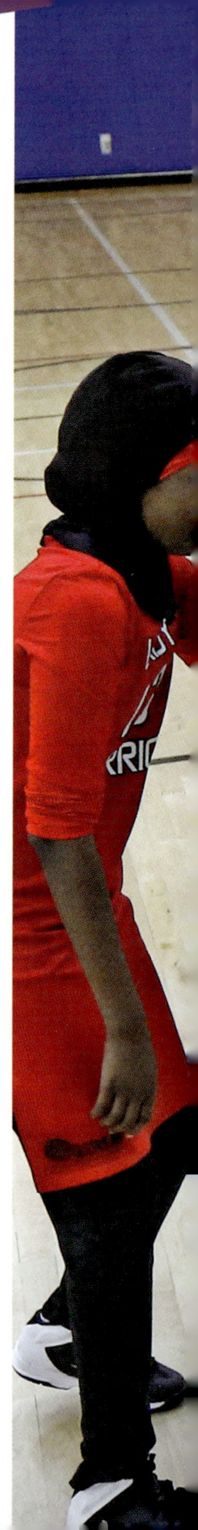

Young Muslim girls wear special uniforms while playing sports. The skirts are shorter so they won't trip. And, their hijabs are fitted so they will not come undone.

FASHION LINE

In 2014, Ibtihaj started a small clothing business with her siblings. The company, called Louella, only sells clothes on the store's website. The collections feature bright colors and updated looks.

Louella is named after Ibtihaj's grandmother. Ibtihaj often wears clothes from her own fashion line.

BUZZ

Ibtihaj feels honored to be a role model. People around the world look up to her. Many hope that she will fence in Tokyo, Japan, for the 2020 Olympics. Fans are excited to see what's next for Ibtihaj Muhammad!

Ibtihaj was named one of *Time* magazine's Most Influential People of 2016.

GLOSSARY

championship a game, a match, or a race held to find a first-place winner. A champion is someone who wins a championship.

coach someone who teaches or trains a person or a group on a certain subject or skill.

foundation (faun-DAY-shuhn) an organization that controls gifts of money and services.

hijab the traditional covering for the hair and neck that is worn by Muslim women.

medal an award for success.

Muslim a person who practices Islam.

scholarship money or aid given to help a student continue his or her studies.

sibling a brother or a sister.

sword a weapon having a long blade usually with a sharp point and edge.

WEBSITES

To learn more about Olympic Biographies, visit **booklinks.abdopublishing.com**. These links are routinely monitored and updated to provide the most current information available.

INDEX